A SIMPLE WISH

The Junior Novelization

A SIMPLE WISH

The Junior Novelization

Adapted by Francine Hughes

Based on the motion picture screenplay
written by Jeff Rothberg

GROSSET & DUNLAP • NEW YORK

Chapter 1

It was the morning of the big exam. A nervous young man hurried into the classroom. He wanted to change jobs. And passing this exam was the way to do it.

The young man gazed at the rows and rows of seats. Dozens of white-haired women sat at desks, already scribbling their answers. He grabbed a test booklet, then sat down.

Whew, he thought. *I know the first answer.*

Name? Murray.

The next one wasn't so easy. Murray straightened his tie. He smoothed back his bright red hair. Then he read the question again.

It didn't do any good.

He looked at a different one. *No*, he told himself. *I'm not sure about that one, either.*

Murray tried the next one, the one after that, and the one after that. No, no, no.

He flipped to the end of the test. Six hundred questions! Murray sat back in his seat. This might take a while.

Hours passed. Day turned into night. Finally Murray filled in the last answer. He put down his pencil and grinned. All things considered, he felt pretty good.

Murray leaned back in his chair to stretch. The chair tipped over, and—thump!—he fell to the ground.

Oliver Greening gripped the reins of his horse-drawn carriage. The horse clip-clopped down a cobblestone path. Trees rose before him. It was quiet. Peaceful.

He straightened his top hat and long black coat. " 'Tis a far, far better thing," he sang with an English accent.

Beep! A horn honked loudly.

"Hey!" Oliver shouted in his regular voice. What did he expect? This was Central Park, New York City. Not some hillside in England.

He shook his fist at a taxi driver. "Look where you're going, you brain-dead animal!"

The horse reared up.

"Relax, Duchess," Oliver said. "I meant that driver. 'Tis a far, far better thing," he sang again.

Oliver was practicing for an audition. A role in a new Broadway show. It was called *Two Cities*, and it was just like the classic Dickens story.

Oliver loved the stage. He loved singing and acting. But his career was in trouble. That's why he drove a horse and carriage—to make money.

Oliver turned his carriage toward the stable. The audition was in a little while. And he had a stop to make first.

"Remember, I'm on a schedule," he told Duchess.

Duchess nodded, then, with a nervous whinny, stopped short. Oliver's hat tumbled off.

"What's the matter, Duchess?" he asked, jumping down from the carriage to get it. "Ah!" he said. A black cat blocked Duchess's way.

Suddenly the cat snarled. Duchess bolted, galloping wildly.

"Stop that horse!" Oliver cried, running after her.

Borrowing a bike from a friend at a hot-dog stand, Oliver took off.

Uphill and down. Around trees and around people. Oliver pedaled hard. He was catching up!

Oliver pulled up alongside Duchess. He let go of the handlebars. Then he grabbed the carriage and kicked the bike away. Finally he pulled himself into the driver's seat. Stretching forward, he grabbed the reins.

Duchess slowed to a trot, then a walk. Oliver glanced at his watch. No time to take Duchess to the stables now. He had more important things to do.

Outside an elementary school, seven-year-old Anabel Greening waited for her dad.

"Hey, Charlie! Guess what?" she said to her older brother.

Charlie bounced a basketball. "I give up," he said, bored.

Anabel wriggled a loose tooth with her tongue. "This tooth is about to go." She brightened. "And I'll get money from the tooth fairy. That will come in handy."

Charlie rolled his eyes. "Tooth fairy! Give me a break." He gazed up the street. "Let's face it. Dad's never going to come." He looked back at Anabel, trying to scare her. "He left us here to rot."

"Did not," Anabel said.

"Did too."

"Did not—see!" Anabel gave Charlie a smug look. "Hi, Dad!" She waved at Oliver coming up the street.

The carriage creaked to a stop in front of the school. Anabel and Charlie climbed aboard.

"Giddyap!" said Oliver. He couldn't change clothes. He couldn't drop off Duchess. He had to go straight to the theater.

It was time for his audition.

Oliver guided Duchess to a stop outside a Broadway theater. Jeri, Oliver's agent, was waiting by the door.

Jeri helped Oliver find acting jobs—not that there'd been many. And now Jeri felt worried. Oliver was six minutes late. And six minutes was really late—at least when the director was Lord Richard.

Lord Richard was a genius, everyone said. Just brilliant. And just as scary, too. Everyone was afraid of him.

Inside the theater, Lord Richard wrung his hands. "My leading man drops out two weeks before we open," he moaned. "I have to find someone new. And…" He held out a cup, looking disgusted. "My tea is too weak!"

His faithful assistant rushed to his side with tea bags.

Lord Richard turned to the stage manager, Manny. "Where's Tony Sable?"

Tony Sable was a famous actor. Already, Lord Richard planned to hire him for the lead.

"He'll be here," Manny told him. "But we have to see Oliver Greening first."

"Who?" asked Lord Richard.

Oliver walked on stage. Lord Richard looked at his top hat and long coat. "You came in costume," he said.

Oliver smiled. "Well, it's a lucky accident."

"Not that lucky," Lord Richard said, tapping his foot. He wanted this audition to be over.

Up in the balcony, Anabel crossed her fingers for luck. Charlie sat next to her.

"Guess what?" he said. "I know something you don't know!"

"Shh," Anabel whispered. "Dad's onstage."

"If Dad doesn't get this part," Charlie went on, "we're moving to Nebraska. To live with Uncle Carl."

"You're lying."

Charlie shook his head. "I heard Dad on the phone. Uncle Carl can give him a job in his factory."

A factory in Nebraska? Anabel thought. *What about Dad's career? What about New York City? And my ballet lessons?*

Onstage, Oliver finished his first song. Then he went on to the next. It was a hard song to sing. The heart and soul of the show.

" 'Tis a far, far better thing…" Oliver's voice rose and fell, filled with emotion.

Anabel and Charlie stopped whispering. Lord Richard stopped drinking his tea. All eyes fastened on Oliver. He was breathtaking. Magical.

Finally Oliver trailed off. He blinked, remembering where he was.

Anabel broke into applause.

The audition was over. Oliver walked offstage. He passed by Tony Sable. Smiling, he tried to say hello.

Tony sneered. He didn't have time for no-name actors. "Nice guys finish last, Greening," he warned Oliver. "And you're one of the nicest guys in town."

It was true. Oliver was nice. And he knew he'd never get the role. Lord Richard wouldn't take a chance on a no-name actor.

So that night Oliver explained everything to Anabel and Charlie. He wasn't making it in New York. The audition he had today? It was his last. Money was tight. And the family needed a good solid home. They were going to move to Nebraska.

Oliver called Uncle Carl to make plans. Grumbling, Charlie helped Anabel get ready for bed.

He opened Anabel's favorite book, *Cinderella*. Then he read it out loud as quickly as he could.

"And so, with the help of her fairy godmother," Charlie said, closing the book, "Cinderella lived unhappily ever after."

"It's *happily*," Anabel corrected. She reached for the book. Then she opened it to a picture of the fairy god-mother.

The fairy godmother had soft white hair, big buckled boots, and a long black coat.

"Charlie?" Anabel asked. "Do you believe in fairy god-mothers?"

Charlie clicked off the light. "I hate to break it to you. But there are no fairy godmothers. No angels. And no tooth fairies."

"You're wrong!" Anabel exclaimed. She took a pretty box from her nightstand. Inside were all her precious treasures. She kept her tooth fairy money right on top. *I'd like Charlie to explain that!* she thought.

Anabel dug a little deeper. She touched a soft pretty ribbon and stroked it gently.

The ribbon was extra-special. Anabel's mom had given it to her before she died.

Then Anabel took out a photograph. A beautiful woman smiled out from the picture. She wore a white gown like Cinderella. She looked like a princess.

She was Anabel's mom.

Chapter 2

Late the next afternoon, office workers streamed out of skyscrapers. People crowded onto subways and buses.

A street musician closed her violin case. She gripped the bow tightly. Then she headed for a small gray building.

A homeless woman clutched a stick. She walked into that same building. So did a business woman...a sales clerk...a police officer.

Throughout the city...in taxis...on bicycles...on foot, women came to this building, holding sticks.

Some sticks were long. Others short. Some had jewels, others glass crystals or golden ornaments. They were smooth, bumpy, thin, and fat.

The sticks were all wands. Magic wands. And the women were heading to NAFGA headquarters: North American Fairy Godmothers Association.

"Check your sticks," a clerk named Rena said as they passed the front desk. "Sign your name in the book. The elevator is on your left."

Hortense, the head fairy godmother, greeted everyone. She had white hair and a warm smile. She looked just like a fairy godmother should.

Hortense led the fairy godmothers to a hidden elevator. Down, down, down they went, way below the street. They entered a room as big as Central Park. Its ceiling seemed to be glass. Stars and lights twinkled everywhere.

The fairy godmothers talked and laughed. Hortense looked around. Everyone was here, except one. The fairy godmother from District 17.

Hortense sighed. Maybe accepting that fairy godmother hadn't been a good idea after all.

Upstairs, a tall blonde woman strode past Rena. She wore a long black dress and sunglasses. A thin, timid girl with shaggy hair followed at her heels.

"Claudia!" Rena cried. She blocked her way. "Hortense took away your wand. You're not a fairy godmother anymore. You can't come in."

Claudia lifted her sunglasses. "But I did come in," she

said sweetly. She nodded toward her friend. "This is my faithful companion, Boots."

"Right, right, right," Boots agreed.

Rena whispered, "I hear you're a witch now."

"You can't be serious." Claudia giggled. Boots barked with laughter.

"But you still have to go," Rena insisted. She picked up the intercom to call Hortense.

"Okay, okay. I'll go," Claudia promised. "But first I have a treat for you." She held out a shiny red apple. It looked delicious. So delicious, Rena had to take a bite.

"Now, is that the apple of a witch?" Claudia asked.

Rena fell over her desk, sound asleep.

"You bet it is!" Claudia answered herself gleefully. She turned to Boots. "Now let's find those wands!"

Anabel was fast asleep. Charlie was in the bed across the room, snoring loudly.

Suddenly Anabel woke up. She felt someone else in the room. Someone watching her. A shadow crossed her bed. It looked like a fairy godmother—holding a magic wand!

Anabel grinned and flicked on a small lamp.

The smile faded.

There stood a nervous-looking young man with red hair. The same red-haired, nervous-looking young man who had been late for the exam—Murray.

"This is apartment 3B, right?" he asked. He checked a little notebook.

The man seemed nice. Anabel wasn't scared at all. So she nodded.

"Good. I would have been here sooner. But I went to the wrong apartment." Murray paused. "It's a common mistake for a fairy godmother."

This guy was a fairy godmother? Anabel looked at him, confused.

"Well, not that common," Murray went on. "But it happens…sometimes. Okay, not often. Okay, okay. Hardly ever."

Anabel sat up. She examined him closely. "You don't look like a fairy godmother."

"I don't?" said Murray. "Is it because I'm tall?"

Anabel shook her head.

"It's the hair, then. Mine's red. Not white."

"No, it's not the hair," Anabel said.

"Not the hair?" Murray repeated.

"You're a guy," Anabel finally said.

"Oh, that." Murray shuffled his feet. "The guy thing. I asked to be called a fairy godfather. But I guess it's a tradition."

"But the one in *Cinderella*…" Anabel trailed off.

Murray shrugged. "What's the difference? As long as there's magic. As long as the person can do the job."

"Can you?" asked Anabel.

Murray didn't answer the question. He gazed at Anabel's doll collection as if it were the most interesting thing in the world. "Look at those dolls!" he exclaimed. Then he tripped and knocked them down. "Oops!" he said.

Quickly, Murray tried to put them back in place. "There you go." He jumbled them all together. "Neat and tidy."

Anabel sighed. This fairy godmother was so nervous, she wanted to help him. "What's your name?" she asked.

"Murray."

Murray? Anabel giggled. What kind of name was that for a fairy godmother?

Murray coughed. In the next bed, Charlie rolled over.

"Who's the joker in the jammies?" Murray asked.

"My brother, Charlie," Anabel answered. "He doesn't believe in fairy godmothers."

"Oh yeah?" Murray laughed. "Maybe he'd think twice if we turn him into a frog."

"Do it," Anabel told him.

Murray gave his wand a practice wave. "A nice simple wish. Consider it done."

This was Murray's first official wish since he passed the test. He flexed his fingers. He stretched his arms. But he couldn't hide the doubt in his eyes. "Now there's only one wish to a customer," he told Anabel. "I just say my spell word, 'Shh-boom,' and…" He brought up his wand.

"Wait!" Anabel cried. "I have a better wish! It's for my dad."

But Murray had already stopped the magic. He'd spotted a calendar. In a panic, he dropped his wand. He grabbed the calendar from Anabel's desk. "Today's Wednesday!" he exclaimed.

Anabel picked up the wand as Murray edged toward the door. "You'll have to take a rain check," he told her. "Right now all the fairy godmothers are at this meeting. Except me. I can just imagine what they're saying."

"But my wish!" Anabel interrupted. "It can't wait. It's—"

Footsteps sounded in the hall.

"Shh," Murray whispered. He stepped back into the shadows. "Make like you're sleeping."

Anabel curled up under the covers. Oliver came into the room. He pulled the blanket up to Charlie's chin. Then he checked on Anabel. He smoothed down her long brown hair. Satisfied everything was fine, he tiptoed out of the room.

Anabel's eyes snapped open. She sat up quickly and looked around. Murray was gone.

And she had his magic wand!

At fairy godmother headquarters, Claudia dragged Boots into room after room. Finally she found what she wanted—a chest filled with magic wands.

Claudia took one end, Boots the other. They began to drag it away.

Suddenly Hortense stepped in their path. "Claudia! What are you doing here?"

"I'm taking what belongs to me," Claudia snapped. "And then some."

"Your wand?" said Hortense. "You were using it for your own selfish needs. That's why I took it away. That's not what fairy godmothers are all about."

"Mostly you're all about seventy," Claudia shot back.

Hortense spied her own wand on top of the pile. She lunged for it.

"Don't even think about it!" cried Claudia. She raised her arm. Sparks flew from her fingertips. Black smoke spiraled through the air. It coiled around Hortense's feet.

They stiffened into cardboard.

The smoke wound around her legs.

They flattened like paper pancakes.

The blackness whirled around her body...her arms...her head.

Hortense turned into a living, breathing, cardboard cutout!

She tried to move her cardboard lips. "You're making a big mistake," she mumbled.

Claudia wriggled her fingers. Whoosh! Bricks rocketed across the room. They landed in Hortense's mouth, building a tiny brick wall.

"That will shut you up." Claudia checked her watch. "For twenty-four hours. That's all I need. And then you and your pals will be out on the street, wondering where the magic went."

Claudia strode to the elevator. She had one thing left to do. She zapped the elevator button. Z-z-z-z-z! The button sizzled. Below, the elevator clanked once. Then it was silent.

Claudia had blown its fuse.

And all the fairy godmothers were still downstairs. Prisoners.

At same moment, Anabel poked her head out of

the bedroom. She walked up to Oliver, who was reading the newspaper.

"My fairy godmother came to see me," Anabel told him.

Smiling, Oliver put down the paper. "Was she nice?"

"Yup. But it was a guy named Murray." Anabel climbed into Oliver's lap. She showed him the magic wand. "He left this. I'm not sure how it works. He had to go away."

Oliver nodded, not believing a word of it. "Maybe if you go back to sleep, he'll come again."

"Nice try, Dad," Anabel said with a laugh. "But I'm not a bit sleepy."

She waved the wand. "Shh-boom! There, I put a spell on you. To help you get the part."

"Come, love." Oliver scooped her up, then carried her to the bedroom. "It's time to sleep."

"Dad?" said Anabel while Oliver tucked her in. "Remember you said Mom went to heaven? That she's an angel now? Were you making it up?"

In bed, Charlie opened one eye. He shut it before Anabel or Oliver could see.

"No," said Oliver. "I wasn't making it up. I believe she's in heaven. But I also think there's a part of her right here."

"Where?" asked Anabel.

"When I look at you...when I look at Charlie...I see her." Oliver gave Anabel a kiss good night.

At NAFGA headquarters, Murray knocked on the door.

No one answered.

That's weird, Murray thought. *Somebody is always here. And with the meeting, all the fairy godmothers should be here.*

Murray banged again and again. The door was covered by a gate. And he couldn't reach the knob. He peered through the window. But he couldn't see a thing.

Murray had to get inside. He had to join the others, show everyone he was a responsible fairy godmother. A good fairy godmother. If only he could open the door....

Murray turned around. He backed in between the gate bars. He squeezed himself through inch by inch.

One arm. The other arm. The back of his head...ears. Now, if he could reach that knob. Almost...almost...

"Uh-oh," Murray said. He was stuck, his face pressed between the bars.

Chapter 3

The next morning, Anabel, Charlie, and Oliver were leaving the apartment when Jeri came up to them.

Anabel crossed her fingers. They'd find out about the audition now. And they needed as much luck as they could get.

Jeri looked at the sidewalk. "I wanted to tell you in person," she began.

Anabel's heart sank. This didn't sound good. She took Oliver's hand.

"I know," said Oliver. "I didn't get the part."

"Not yet." Jeri grinned. "But they want to see you again. Tonight, nine-thirty! You're so close to getting it!"

Anabel gazed at the wand. She did use it last night. "Maybe it's working," she whispered.

"What's working?" Charlie asked. He made a grab for the wand. "Worried I won't give it back?" he teased.

Anabel hesitated. "Okay," she said, deciding to trust him. "But be careful."

Charlie took the wand. "Stupid piece of junk," he muttered.

"No, it's not," Anabel said. She reached to take it back. "It's a magic wand."

Laughing, Charlie waved it over his head. He pretended to hold it out for Anabel. Then he snatched it away. He took one step back. Another step back. He waved it again. "Look at me! I'm making magic!"

Behind Charlie, rows of fruits and vegetables were on display in front of a market.

Charlie wasn't looking where he was going. And he was headed for the apples and red peppers!

"Charlie, watch out!" Anabel shouted.

Bang! Boom! Charlie lost his footing. Smash! He barreled into a stand of veggies. Cardboard and cabbages flew everywhere. Charlie hit the sidewalk, nearly invisible under a pile of peppers and potatoes.

Anabel held her breath. Then Charlie's head popped up. In a daze, he got to his feet. The grocer shook his fist at Charlie, then went to work, cleaning everything up.

"Where's my wand?" Anabel demanded.

Charlie knelt, picking something up from the pavement. He held up half the wand. Then he held up the other half.

The magic wand had snapped in two.

Anabel stuffed the pieces in her bookbag. "I hate you, Charlie!" she shouted.

In the shadow of the Brooklyn Bridge...hidden by wild, wild weeds...behind a high iron fence...sat an old broken-down mansion.

Shutters dangled from windows. The rusty gate creaked open and shut.

In the parlor, Claudia bent over the chest full of wands. "Two hundred and forty-six," she counted. Her blonde hair swung back and forth. "Two hundred and forty-seven."

A portrait hung above the fireplace. A young Claudia sat with a little puppy in her lap. There was something familiar about the dog. She was thin and timid, with shaggy fur—just like Boots.

Boots watched Claudia carefully. She chewed on her knuckles. She scratched behind her ear. She gave a sniff.

Annoyed, Claudia shot her a look.

"Sit!" Claudia commanded.

Boots stared at Claudia like a devoted puppy. "I'm your best friend, right?" she asked.

Claudia nodded. "Now go. Sit."

"But I don't get something," Boots continued. "How come we need all these wands? I mean, you have so much power already."

Claudia paced in front of the fire. "It's not enough," she explained. "To be monstrously evil, I must control white magic, too. Every person in this city has a desperate wish. A secret desire. When I destroy all these goody-goody sticks, they'll have to come to me."

"Right, right," Boots agreed. She squirmed with happiness.

Claudia started counting again. She clenched her teeth. "I don't see it. It's not here. We're one wand short."

Boots sniffed around the empty chest. She pulled out a book. The sign-in book!

Grinning, Claudia snatched it from Boots's hands. She flipped through the pages. Every fairy godmother was listed. Except for one.

"The Seventeenth District!" Claudia exclaimed. "That was my territory."

"We can sniff it out," Boots put in helpfully.

Claudia drew back, a little afraid. "I haven't been out in broad daylight for years."

Then she checked her magic mirror hanging on the

wall. The reflection looked like the Claudia in the portrait. Young and pretty. Claudia smiled.

"Fetch my coat," she ordered Boots.

Anabel sat in art class, her supplies spread out before her.

"Remember," Ms. Bramble said in a harsh voice, "our napkin holders must be finished today." She strode up the aisles. "Too much glue," she told one girl. "Not enough glue," she said to a boy.

Anabel bent over her project. Glue, tape. What else would keep the wand together?

"What's this?" Ms. Bramble loomed over. "That's not our assignment. Now hand over your toy."

Anabel gripped the wand tightly. "It's not a toy," she explained. "It's a magic wand."

"Of course," Ms. Bramble said sweetly. "Now give it over," she ordered.

The wand belonged to Murray. No one else could have it. Anabel leaped up. She bolted into the hallway.

"Anabel!" Ms. Bramble shouted, giving chase.

Anabel ducked behind an open door. She stood quietly, not making a sound.

Footsteps thudded down the hall. The sound grew fainter and fainter. Ms. Bramble had passed right by.

Anabel sighed with relief. Then she caught her breath. More footsteps…coming closer…closer…

The footsteps stopped—right outside.

Anabel saw a pair of shoes. She looked up.

"Murray!" she cried.

"Anabel!" Murray said, hurrying closer. "Thank goodness I found you."

Anabel gazed at her fairy godmother. "Where have you been?" she asked.

"It's a long story," Murray replied, "involving the police, the fire department, and an iron gate. By any chance, did I leave my—"

Anabel held up the broken wand, a sad expression on her face.

Murray took it carefully. "Oh, my. This is bad," he said.

"I tried gluing it back together," Anabel told him.

Murray slumped down next to Anabel. "You get one wand," he said, upset. "It's supposed to last forever."

Anabel felt terrible. Quickly she untied her hair ribbon. It was her lucky ribbon—the one her mom had given her. She tied the ribbon around the popsicle sticks alongside the wand.

"This will keep the pieces together until the glue dries," she said.

Murray looked at it doubtfully. "I'll still do what I can to grant your wish," he told her. "But no guarantees."

Anabel pulled Murray to his feet, and they started down the hall. "This wish," she explained, "the future of my entire family depends on it."

"Great." Murray gave a short laugh. "No pressure."

"Okay," Anabel continued. She stopped inside the school entrance. "My dad has to sing tonight. If he does it better than anyone else, he'll get this part. And we won't have to move to Nebraska with Uncle Carl. He won't have to work in the factory and—"

Murray held up his hand. "Keep it simple," he warned. There was no telling what would happen with a complicated wish.

"I wish my dad gets the part. Can you do it?"

Murray gazed around the school lobby. Children's drawings and paintings decorated the walls. "Not here," he said. "I have to be close to the wishee—your dad."

"He's by Central Park," Anabel said. "Outside the Plaza Hotel. Come on! The subway is two blocks away."

Murray stopped her. He waved his wand. "Who needs the subway?"

Anabel brightened. She'd get to see some magic right away!

"But I can't do this alone," Murray continued. "Picture the place you want to be."

Anabel locked eyes with Murray. Murray grasped the wand like an orchestra conductor. "Shh-boooom!" he said—just as Ms. Bramble appeared.

A gust of wind blew through the lobby.

"Anabel Greening, get back here," Ms. Bramble ordered.

The wind grew stronger. Faster. Anabel's hair streamed straight out. The drawings were torn from the walls. Pictures swirled in the air. They whipped around and around like a paper tornado, surrounding Anabel and Murray.

A desk chair whooshed into the lobby. It rolled faster and faster…right into Ms. Bramble.

Plop! She fell into the seat. The chair careened backward.

Ms. Bramble covered her eyes. She was zooming down the hallway!

The chair bumped against a wall. The wind died down. The papers fluttered for a moment. Then they floated down to the floor.

"Anabel?" Ms. Bramble looked up. Down. And under her chair.

Anabel and Murray had disappeared.

Chapter 4

It was quiet. *Too quiet for New York City*, Anabel thought. And all she could see was blackness.

She pulled a picture off her face. There! Blue sky. Green grass. Empty space as far as she could see. And Murray, crumpled on the ground.

Anabel hurried to his side. Murray groaned as he took in the view.

Definitely not New York City, Anabel thought.

"Looks like I missed an off-ramp," Murray said, sitting up.

Anabel scooped up the broken wand and handed it to Murray. They needed to get going. They needed to figure out where they were.

Anabel spied a building in the distance. She helped Murray up, and they began to walk.

"Nebraska," Murray said, reading a sign on the road.

They were in Nebraska!

Anabel and Murray neared the building. Anabel could see it was old. Falling apart.

Murray read the graying sign: "The Plaza Motel."

The Plaza Motel in Nebraska? A wave of disappointment hit Anabel. She gazed at Murray. His red hair stood on end. His clothes were dusty. And his wand was still broken in two.

Maybe he wasn't much of a fairy godmother after all.

"Anabel?" said Murray. "When I told you to get a picture in your head, what did you think? Did you have Nebraska on your mind?"

Anabel shuffled her feet. She kicked up a cloud of dust.

"Well, a little," she admitted. Then she stood up straight. "Are you saying this is my fault? You're the guy who did it. You and your no-good magic wand."

"Which was fine until you broke it."

"Which wouldn't be broken if you hadn't forgotten it."

"Hey," said Murray, "if you had let me turn Charlie into a frog, none of this would have happened."

"Oh!" Anabel stamped her foot. "Can't you just say you blew it?"

"Did not," said Murray.

"Did too."

"Did not."

"Did too to infinity," Anabel shot back.

"Did not to…oh, okay." Murray sighed. "You're right. It's all my fault. The other fairy godmothers are right. A guy can't make it. I give up."

"You can't give up," Anabel told Murray. "I won't let you."

Back at school, Charlie was searching for Anabel. She was supposed to meet him outside. And it wasn't like her to be late.

He edged up to a crowd inside the lobby. A doctor was taking Ms. Bramble's pulse.

"What's going on?" Charlie asked a girl from Anabel's class.

"Ms. Bramble went mental," the girl answered. "And Anabel ran away."

"Yeah," added another girl, giggling. "She took her magic wand."

"I saw it!" Ms. Bramble suddenly cried. "The girl flew away! She did!" She clutched the doctor's arm. "You have to believe me."

Anabel! Charlie thought. He suddenly felt sick. Sure he liked to tease Anabel and pretend he didn't like her. But that's all it was. Pretend.

A bright splash of color caught his eye. Something was fluttering in the ceiling vent. Charlie reached for it.

It was Anabel's ribbon.

In a flash, Charlie slipped on his rollerblades. He had to find Oliver. And fast!

Not far away, Claudia scoured the streets. She held her District 17 guidebook in one hand. It listed all the kids in the territory. Frowning, she crossed off another address. None of these kids had seen a fairy godmother.

There was only one address left. Claudia glanced up. It was this building, right here. The kid's name: Anabel Greening.

Boots panted over Claudia's shoulder. She sniffed. "I think…" She sniffed again. "Yes. I knew it. It's close by. My nose led us to it. It's—"

"Boots!" Claudia interrupted. "It's the only address left."

No one was home. So they sneaked inside the apartment. Boots padded down the hall. She picked up a picture of Anabel dressed for a dance recital.

"She's a ballerina," Claudia sneered. "How cute." She kicked Anabel's book across the floor. "Cinderella!" She gagged. "I hate that story."

Just then the phone rang. The answering machine clicked on. "Oliver?" Jeri's voice floated through the apartment. "Your audition is on for tonight. Nine-thirty at the Palace Theater."

The Palace? Claudia had to laugh. Cinderella went to the palace because of her fairy godmother. She got her wish. But it wasn't going to happen for Anabel.

"Bootsie," she said, "would you like to dress up and go to the Palace?"

Anabel found a phone beside the old motel. *Great*, she thought. *We'll find a way to get home now. We'll be back by tonight. In time for Dad's audition.*

She pressed her ear to the receiver.

No dial tone.

Murray showed her the cord. It was broken.

Bang! A gunshot rang out. Murray jumped. Anabel screamed.

"You're on my property," a man shouted. He stomped closer.

Anabel gasped. The man was big and mean-looking, and he carried a shotgun. She ducked behind Murray.

"Greetings, friend." Murray held out his hand to shake.

The man spat.

"Lovely hobby," Murray said warmly. "My name's Murray. This is Anabel. And you are—"

The man just stared.

Murray spied a name stitched on the man's dirty shirt. "Ah!" he said. "You must be Roy. I always liked the name Roy. Roy, Roy, Roy. It rolls right off the tongue."

"It ain't Roy," the man said finally. "It ain't my shirt."

"Good," Murray told him quickly. "Roy is a terrible name for a big guy like you. Roy, Roy…it sounds like toy."

The man pulled open the shirt. A tattoo was etched into his chest: a skull and crossbones, and the name Duane.

"That's very artistic, Duane," Murray said.

Duane spat again. He eyed the magic wand. "What's that?"

"It's a magic wand," Anabel cried out. "And it's more powerful than your stupid shotgun."

Duane stomped closer. "Gimme," he grunted.

"Sorry." Murray tried to sound as tough as Duane. "I can't give it up. It's too powerful."

Duane stood inches away. "What are you going to do? Turn me into a little rabbit?"

"Is that your wish?" Murray asked.

"Yeah. Take your best shot." Duane patted his gun. "Then I'll take mine."

Murray pieced together the wand. *Here goes nothing,* he thought.

"Shhh-booom!"

The wind kicked up. Dust spun around and around… circling Duane. But instead of becoming a tiny little rabbit, Duane grew larger and larger. He became a giant rabbi! Murray's spell didn't quite work.

Murray grabbed Anabel's hand, and they raced for the road.

"Anabel, quick!" he cried. "Wish New York City. Central Park. Think Central Park!"

Anabel squeezed her eyes shut. She thought and thought and thought.

"Shhh-boooom!"

A moment later, Murray and Anabel saw green fields. Skyscrapers. Central Park!

I did it, Murray thought. *I really did it!*

Suddenly he heard a seal bark. Murray gazed around. They'd landed on the seal island at the zoo.

Splat! A fish hit him in the face.

It was feeding time.

Chapter 5

Anabel and Murray sped through the park. They had to find Oliver and cast the wish. Finally they saw him across a pond. He was showing some tourists a row of statues.

"All right," Murray said. "Let's do this."

He limbered up, cracking his knuckles. Then he shrugged his shoulders to loosen the muscles.

"I take pride in my job," Murray continued. "And I'll get this wish right if it kills me. Okay, Anabel. See it in your head. See your wish coming true."

Anabel shut her eyes. Murray raised his wand. He swept it in a circle. Then he aimed it across the water at Oliver. "Shhh-booom!"

Anabel caught her breath and waited. Nothing happened.

Then suddenly, a huge gust of wind sprang up.

Newspapers swirled all around. The tourists held on to their coats. People screamed and grabbed their dogs' leashes.

Oliver held his hat to keep it in place. But the wind was too strong. WHOOSH! Off it blew.

Bright sparkling stars spun around the hat. Amazed, Oliver clutched it. The stars whirled around his ears…along his arms…down to his toes. They spun around Duchess…up her legs…around her tail…and onto the carriage.

Murray dropped his arm. The wind died away. It was over. Anabel opened her eyes. She didn't see Oliver. Or Duchess. Or the carriage. She saw only the tourists, standing around a big orange pumpkin.

Anabel and Murray raced around the pond. "Dad?" Anabel called. "Where did you go?"

"Anabel!" Charlie screeched to a stop on his rollerblades. "What's going on?" he demanded. He peered at Murray. "Who is this?"

"Murray," answered Anabel. "My fairy godmother."

Charlie laughed.

Murray drew himself up. "You could be a frog right now," he told Charlie. "Besides, 'fairy godmother' is only a job description. I prefer 'magic-wand operator.' "

Charlie laughed again, not believing it for a second. A

mouse scurried toward them. "Eek!" screamed a tourist.

Anabel knelt beside the frightened little mouse. She gazed at the tiny horse collar around her neck.

"It's Duchess!" she exclaimed.

"Duchess?" Charlie repeated.

"Neigh!" whinnied the mouse.

Anabel opened her bookbag. "You'll be safe here," she told the mouse. Duchess scampered inside.

Maybe it is Duchess, Charlie thought. He turned to Murray. "I'm not saying I believe you're a fairy godmother. But what's going on? And where's Dad?"

Anabel stood up. She knew where their father was. She pointed in front of her.

Murray gazed anxiously at one of the bronze statues. It wore a top hat, a long coat—and a very surprised expression. It was Oliver Greening!

Anabel's dad had an audition in just a few hours. And he was a statue. Murray needed help.

"I need Hortense," he told Anabel and Charlie. Quickly he led them to fairy godmother headquarters.

"I think I can explain," he said, hurrying down the street. "When I asked you to see the wish, did you think about Cinderella?"

Anabel nodded.

"So," Murray continued, "the carriage became a pumpkin. The horse a mouse."

"It's like Cinderella. But backwards!" Anabel exclaimed. "So at midnight, Dad will turn back to normal, just like the book! The spell will be over." She paused to look at Murray. "Won't it?"

Murray couldn't meet her eyes. He didn't know. "Good question," he told her, gazing up the street.

In a few minutes, they reached headquarters. Murray tried the door. It was still locked up tight.

Murray and Charlie stared at the gate, not knowing what to do. Anabel decided to climb.

"Give me a boost," she told them.

Charlie helped her onto Murray's shoulders. Then he passed her the ribbon for luck. Anabel placed it in her pocket. She pushed herself to the top of the gate and leaped onto the window ledge.

A second later she tumbled into the building.

Inside, Anabel dusted herself off. She scurried past the cardboard Hortense…past Rena sleeping at the desk.

Finally she let Murray and Charlie in the front door.

Mmf. Mmf. Murray stopped in his tracks. What was that noise? It sounded like muffled breathing. *Mmf. Mmf.*

"Hortense!" cried Murray. He ran over to the cardboard figure. He gazed at Hortense, flat as a pancake with bricks in her mouth. He had to do something…something magical.

"Hortense! Yoo-hoo!" Murray raised his wand. Anabel and Charlie ducked behind the couch.

Murray shot them a dirty look. But he had a job to do. A fairy godmother to save. He flexed his fingers, warming up. He stretched and bent, and bent and stretched. And then he did it some more.

At last he waved his magic wand and said, "Shhhbooom!"

The bricks burst out one by one.

Murray smiled, pleased. Hortense's mouth was free. He could work on unflattening her later.

Rena appeared in the doorway, yawning. "Hello, Murray," she said.

Hortense coughed up brick dust. "We don't have time for small talk," she snapped. "We have a crisis on our hands." She eyed Murray's broken wand. "Get to work on it, Rena," she ordered. "We need that wand."

Rena yanked Murray along with her, and Murray yanked Charlie.

Rena bent over the wand. She called for a drill. A glue gun. She put on a huge safety helmet. Then she went to work.

Meanwhile, Hortense told Anabel all about Claudia,

and then Anabel told Hortense everything that had happened in the park.

"Ah, 'the Cinderella variation'…. This is not easy to fix." Hortense sighed. "Even for an experienced fairy godmother. It's not enough for Murray to trust the spells. He has to trust himself. With no hesitation. But he'll make it. I have faith."

Anabel nodded. "He's really a good person."

"Yes," Hortense agreed. "But if Murray doesn't complete your wish, he's finished as a fairy godmother. And no one can help him. The other fairy godmothers are stuck downstairs without their wands."

Anabel looked worried but determined. Her father was a statue in Central Park. And it seemed as if no one could do anything about it.

"Now, now, dear," Hortense said gently. "There's always hope. But before I can help you, you have to help me…. Get the wands. Save the world."

When Rena finished the wand, it was already quarter after nine. Only fifteen more minutes until Oliver's audition.

Murray tried to concentrate. Anabel had promised Hortense they'd get the wands. But how would they find Claudia? And what about Oliver?

"There must be something you can do to get more time," Anabel said to Murray.

Murray looked at her thoughtfully. Maybe there was a way.

They rushed to the theater. Inside, Tony Sable stood onstage.

"Ladies and gentlemen," Lord Richard announced to the cast and crew, "it gives me great pleasure to introduce you to the star of my twenty-third consecutive hit!"

It's not over yet, Anabel thought, leading Murray to the balcony.

They gazed down to the stage. The spotlight fell on Tony. He bowed. Then he opened his mouth, about to sing.

"What if…" Murray whispered. "You know the feeling you get with a sore throat? Kind of scratchy?"

"Like a frog in your throat?" Anabel asked, gazing at him uncertainly. It seemed simple enough. But so did getting to the Plaza Hotel. "Think you can do it?"

"What kind of question is that?" Murray asked. Then he sighed and answered his own question. "A very good one, actually."

Anabel thought about Hortense. About Murray trusting himself. "You can do it," she told him. "You can do anything!" She pulled out her hair ribbon. "My mom gave me this for luck. Take it."

40

Would a hair ribbon do much good? Murray shrugged. It certainly couldn't hurt. And it was awfully sweet.

He closed his eyes and waved his newly fixed wand. "Shh-boooom!"

Onstage, Tony began to sing. " 'Tis—" A cough choked off the rest. Tony shut his mouth. The coughing stopped.

He nodded, ready to try again. " 'Tis—" Cough, cough. He doubled over. Cough. He opened his mouth wide. And a frog jumped out onto the piano.

Everyone gasped.

"Yes!" cried Murray. "I did it! The man with the wand is back!"

Cough, cough. Another frog hopped out. And another.

Frog after frog sprang out of Tony Sable's mouth. They filled the aisles. They jumped from seat to seat. Croaking. Leaping. People ran, screaming, from the theater.

Anabel smiled as the people fled. Nothing else would be done today. Tony Sable might still get the part. But at least no one would notice that Oliver had missed his audition.

Anabel looked at Murray admiringly. "When I grow up," she told him, "I want to be a fairy godmother."

Murray beamed at her. Then he held out his wand. "I shouldn't let you do this…" He trailed off. But why not? What harm could it do?

Anabel held the wand carefully. Murray wrapped his hand around hers. He showed her the moves. They swayed back. They lunged forward—

"Oh!" cried Anabel. The wand flew out of her hand. It soared up, up, up…then over the balcony railing.

Anabel peered over the ledge. Where did it fall?

Suddenly Boots grabbed her from behind. She clapped a hand over Anabel's mouth.

Murray gasped. "Let her go!" he demanded. He leaped to Anabel's rescue.

"Back off, Murray," ordered Boots. "Or I'll push her over."

Murray backed off.

"Now, where's Claudia's wand?"

No one answered.

Boots spied Anabel's bookbag on the ground. Still holding Anabel, she stuck her head in the bag.

Downstairs, Charlie waved up at Murray. He had something in his hand. The wand!

"Mm-mmm," Boots said, pulling Duchess out of the bag. "I'm so hungry I could eat a horse." She smacked her lips.

"No!" Anabel twisted, trying to break free.

Murray thought quickly. Maybe he could still save Oliver…and Duchess…and get the wands back, too.

"You don't scare us," Murray told Boots. "Claudia does. But not you."

He nodded for Anabel to follow his lead.

"Yeah," Anabel added. "Claudia is scary."

"She could get it out of us," Murray continued. "But you wouldn't take us there. That's too cruel."

"Please," begged Anabel, "don't take us to Claudia."

Boots snickered. "You know what? I'm taking you to Claudia."

Suddenly Duchess strained forward. She nipped Boots on the finger.

"Ow!" Boots dropped the mouse, and Duchess scampered down to Charlie.

Boots started after her. Then she changed her mind. She didn't want to keep Claudia waiting.

Boots pushed Murray and Anabel to the exit.

Chapter 6

At Claudia's mansion, Boots brought Anabel and Murray into the ballroom. High windows lined the walls. Anabel gazed up. Dark clouds were moving in.

Boots chewed on a sock. She eyed Claudia nervously.

"I told you to bring back one measly wand," Claudia hissed. "And you failed."

Murray nudged Anabel. He nodded toward the box of wands in the hallway. "I just need a chance," Murray whispered.

"Eh?" Claudia strode over. "Care to share it with the rest of the class?" She cupped Anabel's face in her hands. "Where is my wand?"

"Don't talk to her, Anabel!" warned Murray. "Don't even look at her."

"Anabel," Claudia continued in a gentle voice, "do you like Cinderella?"

Surprised, Anabel shifted her gaze to Claudia.

"It's all right," Claudia told her sweetly. "I do too. Now, make a wish. Any wish."

"Don't do it!" Murray shouted. "It's a trick."

Anabel clamped her mouth shut.

Impatient, Claudia stamped her foot. "Then I will choose for you! This child wishes—"

"To be a great dancer?" Boots said, remembering the picture of Anabel's recital.

Anabel's eyes opened wide.

"Aha!" said Claudia. She swept her arms out toward Anabel. Dark bolts of lightning shot out, twisting, spinning…circling Anabel's feet.

Anabel gazed down. She was wearing ballet shoes.

Claudia tossed another bolt. Crack! It hit a music box with a teeny-tiny orchestra. The musicians came to life, filling the ballroom with music.

Anabel rose up on her toes like a puppet on a string. She started to dance. She pirouetted, leaped, and twirled.

"I can't stop!" she cried.

"Oh, but you can," Claudia told her. "Just tell me where the wand is."

Anabel shook her head.

Do it now, Murray told himself. *While Claudia isn't looking.* He edged toward the wands, out into the hall.

Not taking her eyes off Anabel, Claudia threw back her arm. Black smoke whirled from her fingertips... across the ballroom...around the corner...into the hallway.

"Oooww!" Murray screamed. He danced back into the room wearing tights and ballet slippers. He twirled and spun toward Anabel. She leaped into his arms for a graceful lift.

Anabel breathed hard. She was getting tired. Claudia waved her fingers, and the music sped up. Their feet flew, quicker and quicker. Anabel and Murray whirled around the room. They could not get at the wands now. But Murray had another idea. He whispered in Anabel's ear. Anabel nodded.

Suddenly an ear-piercing shriek cut through the music.

"I give up!" Anabel screamed. "I'll tell everything."

Claudia grinned. The music stopped. Murray and Anabel spun to a standstill.

"Anabel, don't!" Murray shouted. He reached out for her. But she squirmed out of his grasp.

46

Claudia turned to Boots. "Guard him," she ordered. Then she led Anabel into the parlor.

"The wand's in Central Park," Anabel told her quickly. "I'll take you there. But I want something in return."

She told Claudia about her father. How Murray had turned him into a statue. Claudia chuckled, loving every detail. She was beginning to like this little girl.

Anabel went on and on, tattling on Murray's every mistake.

She waved her arm behind her back. Murray nodded. Claudia was distracted. Now he had to take care of Boots.

"Don't try anything," Boots warned. " 'Cause you'll be sorry. I'm going to be a witch. Claudia promised."

Murray shook his head. "You poor mutt. She's lying. She says she's your friend. But she's not."

Boots got a worried look on her face. She thought it over for a few minutes. Finally she moved closer to Claudia in the other room. She cocked her ear, listening to what Claudia was saying.

Creak! Murray heard a window open. He craned his neck toward the sound. Charlie was peering down, into the ballroom. He waved the wand at Murray.

Murray smiled. Charlie had followed them on his rollerblades and still had the wand! Now if only he'd pass it down. Murray motioned for Charlie to drop the wand.

"What?" Charlie mouthed. He leaned forward, trying to understand. Farther and farther he stretched, until…he tumbled through the window!

Charlie grabbed on to the curtain to break his fall. Murray scrambled to get out of the way. But Charlie swung down, right on top of him.

Thud! Boots wheeled around. Claudia rushed in. They saw Murray, looking dazed.

The curtain was bunched up behind him. Charlie hid quietly underneath.

"Trying to leave, Murray?" Claudia sneered. "I thought we were having fun."

Claudia swatted Boots with a rolled up newspaper. "You didn't watch him. Bad Boots. Now drag those wands over to the fire."

Murray watched Claudia pace the floor. She was talking…threatening…but he wasn't listening. He was too nervous. Charlie's elbow pad had come off when he fell. And it was laying right out in the open.

Murray groaned. Claudia hadn't noticed yet. But she'd pace back any minute now. Murray would have to grab her attention. Buy enough time for Anabel to get the wands. Or for Charlie to toss over his.

"I'm going to get rid of all the fairy godmothers," Claudia was saying.

"Get rid of all the fairy godmothers," Murray repeated.

"How dare you mock me!" Claudia said, outraged.

"How dare you mock me!" Murray said, outraged.

"Cut that out!"

"Cut that out!"

"Watch it, Murray!" Claudia warned.

"You don't seem very confident," Murray told her. "Look at those worry lines."

"Worry lines?" Claudia said vainly. "You're lying!"

"No," Murray said. "They're right next to that wart."

Wart! "I could break every bone in your body." Claudia lifted her arm and zapped him.

Murray stood still for an instant. Then he crumpled into a rubbery heap. Every bone in his body was gone.

Claudia zapped him again. Murray flew through the air. Thump! He hit the floor, every bone back in place.

Claudia laughed. "Now is the time for all good men and little girls to spill the beans." Little girl? Claudia turned around quickly. "Anabel!" she cried.

Anabel froze, with one hand hovering over the wands. Claudia stretched her arm, ready to unleash another spell. But just then she kicked Charlie's elbow pad. Curious, she bent to examine it.

Quickly, Charlie slid the wand across the floor toward Murray. The fairy godmother leaned to get it. But Claudia spotted it too. She dove.

"Aha!" they both said, grabbing the wand at once.

Murray tugged it closer. Claudia pulled it back. Back and forth, back and forth it went. Finally Claudia jumped on Murray.

Charlie leaped into the action. He grabbed Claudia's hair.

"Hey!" cried Claudia as the wig flipped off. Shocked, Charlie stood still, clutching the blonde hair. Murray let go of the wand, just as surprised.

Claudia grabbed it.

Snarling, she snatched back the wig. She plopped it on her head. It hung there, lopsided.

"At last!" Claudia shouted. She snapped her fingers at Boots. "Get them into the parlor," she said with a wicked laugh. "Now!"

It was eleven-thirty p.m. Only a half hour to midnight. And what would happen then? Anabel wondered. If

Murray didn't do something, would her dad be frozen forever?

Claudia loomed over the roaring fire. Flames leaped and danced. Lightning lit the room. Thunder rumbled, shaking the old mansion. Boots crouched next to the chest of wands. She looked troubled.

Claudia dangled the wand—Murray's wand—in front of the fire. "Let's start with this one."

"Claudia?" Boots interrupted. "What about me? Aren't I your best friend? Will I be your partner?"

"You?" Claudia exclaimed. "You whine and scratch, and you stink when it rains. You exist because of one weak moment. My cable went out and I needed someone to talk to."

She turned back to the fire, grinning an evil grin. But suddenly she shrieked and dropped the wand. "Ow!"

Boots was biting her ankle. Hard.

The wand rolled near the fire. "Let go!" Claudia cried, sending a bolt of black lightning right at Boots.

Boots huddled close to the ground as the spell struck her. Fur shot up along her face, her hands, her legs. She grew smaller and smaller.

"Woof!" Boots barked.

She was a dog!

Anabel and Charlie watched. What should they do? Grab the wands? Help Murray?

"Go!" Murray shouted to them. "Take the other wands!" He lunged for his own wand. Thump! Claudia's foot came down on Murray's hand. The wand rolled away.

Claudia swooped down to the floor. She crawled for the wand. She was reaching out…she almost had it…

Boots snatched the wand with her teeth.

Claudia approached Boots. "Drop it at my feet," she ordered.

Murray smiled at the little dog. "Come on, Bootsie, want a tummy rub?"

Boots cocked her head, confused. Then she bolted up the grand staircase.

Claudia leaped onto the banister. She summoned her magic and slid up after the dog. In a flash, Boots reeled around and scampered back down.

Thump! The little dog careened into Murray. They teetered in front of the giant mirror.

"Good riddance to you both!" Claudia shouted. She raised her arm. Black lightning hurtled toward Murray and Boots.

Murray grabbed Boots, pushing her out of the way. They rolled across the floor.

Thwack! Claudia's spell hit the mirror. It bounced off, speeding right back to her like a boomerang.

There was no time for Claudia to get out of the way.

The spell hit her. It pulled her across the room…sucking her through the mirror glass.

"No, no, no!" Claudia shrieked, trapped inside. She pounded the glass. "Do something, you idiot," she shouted at Murray.

Murray just grinned at her.

Enraged, Claudia banged the glass harder and harder. The mirror began to shake. It trembled and rattled and tore off the wall.

Crack! Smash! The mirror fell to the floor and shattered into a hundred little bits. Each shard held a part of Claudia, like pieces of a jigsaw puzzle.

Claudia's eyes glared at Murray from one shard. Her fist waved in another.

"Murray!" Claudia's mouth cried out, sounding strange and far away.

Murray ignored the shouts. He and Boots raced outside. It had stopped raining. The street glistened in the moonlight. The storm was over.

A minute later, Murray and Boots caught up with Anabel and Charlie—and the chest of wands.

"Claudia just went to pieces," Murray told them. "And we have ten minutes to make it to the park." He waved his magic wand—at a taxi cab.

"Taxi!" he called.

Chapter 7

At Central Park, a little mouse cautiously scooted around the bright orange pumpkin and scurried over to the row of statues.

"Neigh," the mouse whinnied at Oliver's feet. It was Duchess.

"Meow!" The same black cat that had scared Duchess the day before leaped out from behind a garbage can.

Duchess backed away. The cat followed her, step for step. Suddenly Duchess turned tail. She bolted under a dumpster. The black cat hissed. He circled the dumpster again and again.

Anabel, Murray, and Charlie dashed up to Oliver. Boots followed behind.

Bong, bong. A clock began to chime midnight.

Murray nodded at Anabel. She concentrated hard on her wish, then glanced back at Murray. He seemed strong. Unafraid. But inside, his stomach was tied in knots.

"Shhh-boooom!" he said as the clock finished striking. Nothing happened.

Murray's heart sank. It was over. He had failed.

"That's it," he said sadly. "I got nothing left."

Anabel's eyes flashed. "Listen to me, Murray. We made it this far. You can't quit now."

But Murray didn't know what else to do. "You both deserved better," he told Anabel and Charlie.

Anabel refused to listen. "You gave me one wish. You said to keep it simple. Well, how's this? I wish my father back the way he was. Okay? Nothing else."

"We don't care if he can sing," Charlie pleaded. "Or if we have to move to Nebraska."

"I believe in you," Anabel told Murray.

Murray shrugged. "That makes one of us."

Anabel took Murray's hand. "Let's all hold hands."

Charlie held back a moment. Then he stepped forward. Linking hands, they formed a small circle.

"Now see the wish," Anabel said.

All three concentrated. They pictured Oliver. The way things used to be. Time seemed to stand still. It was just the three of them. And the statue of Oliver. And the magic in the air.

A gentle wind blew through the park. It ruffled the leaves…blew back their hair. The statue rippled like water.

Anabel stared. Was it really changing?

A rumbling loud as thunder rocked the park. Lightning bolts…swirling lines of color…circled the dumpster. The dumpster rattled. It shook. The cat eyed it, fur standing on end.

The dumpster tipped over. "NEIGH!" Duchess the horse reared up, big and strong.

"Meow!" The cat dashed into the woods.

The colors swirled around the pumpkin. The pumpkin changed shape. It was the carriage again!

Anabel and Charlie gazed up at Oliver. Maybe I just imagined him moving, Anabel thought.

The swirling colors disappeared. Oliver still stood without moving. But something was different. The bronze color was fading. Oliver raised one hand.

He was back to normal!

"Dad!" cried Anabel. She ran to him, Charlie at her heels. They flung their arms around their father.

"We got you back!" Charlie shouted. "We did it!"

"Back?" Oliver repeated, confused. "From where?" He

saw Duchess and the carriage nearby. "And what am I doing here—now?"

"It all has to do with Anabel's fairy godmother," Charlie explained.

Oliver winked at Charlie. "Of course," he said, pleased that Charlie wasn't making fun.

Anabel turned to Murray. She wanted to thank him.

But Murray was nowhere in sight.

Chapter 8

It was opening night for *Two Cities*. Anabel and Charlie met Oliver met backstage. He was warming up for his part: one line in the second act.

"Don't forget," Jeri told them. "He's understudy to Tony Sable, too."

Tony sauntered by, his nose in the air.

"Understudy." Oliver laughed. "I'll only get the lead if something happens to Tony. If he kicks the bucket."

A stage hand was placing a bucket onstage. Anabel looked at it, then at Charlie. "Come on," she whispered. "Try a wish. Get a picture in your head."

Tony marched across stage. Behind the curtain, some-one was watching him and waving a battered-looking wand. "Shh-boom." The words were soft. But they were spoken with power and confidence.

Suddenly Tony tripped. He kicked the bucket. Thud! He tumbled to the ground, clutching his leg.

"I'm okay," Tony insisted.

Lord Richard glared at him. This was just the excuse he was looking for. Tony was impossible. And he had another actor who was even better.

"You were never okay," Lord Richard said. "Take his costume. We have a cast change to announce."

Anabel jumped up and down. Oliver was going on! He was going to be a star!

A few moments later, the curtain lifted. Oliver stepped onstage. He sang. He acted. Thunderous applause echoed through the theater.

Anabel turned in her seat and saw Murray in the audience. She blew him a kiss.

People rose to their feet, cheering for Oliver.

Quietly, Murray slipped out the door. Boots was waiting for him outside. Murray patted her head, then picked up her leash. Together they walked down the streets of New York. Proud. Confident. A cute little dog named Boots.

And a fairy godmother named Murray.